D1226453

FLOWER FAIRIES
THE
LITTLE GREEN BOOK

FLOWER FAIRIES
THE
LITTLE GREEN BOOK

CICELY MARY BARKER
FREDERICK WARNE

FREDERICK WARNE

Penguin Books Ltd, Harmondsworth, Middlesex, England
New York, Australia, Canada, New Zealand

First Published 1995
1 3 5 7 9 10 8 6 4 2

ISBN 0 7232 4189 9

Printed and bound by
Tien Wah Press, Singapore

CONTENTS

The Cherry Tree Fairy
The Hazel-Nut Fairy
The Holly Fairy
The Silver Birch Fairy
The Box Tree Fairy
The Ribwort Plantain Fairy
The Horse Chestnut Fairy
The Nightshade Berry Fairy
The Plane Tree Fairy
The Mulberry Fairy
The Burdock Fairy
The Yew Fairy

The Beech Tree Fairy

◆ THE SONG OF ◆
THE BEECH TREE FAIRY

The trunks of Beeches are smooth and grey,
 Like tall straight pillars of stone
In great Cathedrals where people pray;
 Yet from tiny things they've grown.
About their roots is the moss; and wide
 Their branches spread, and high;
It seems to us, on the earth who bide,
 That their heads are in the sky.

And when Spring is here,
 and their leaves appear,
  With a silky fringe on each,
Nothing is seen so new and green
 As the new young green of Beech.
O the great grey Beech is young, is young,
 When, dangling soft and small,
Round balls of bloom from its twigs are hung,
 And the sun shines over all.

◆ THE SONG OF ◆
THE ROSE HIP FAIRY

Cool dewy morning,
  Blue sky at noon,
White mist at evening,
  And large yellow moon;

Blackberries juicy
  For staining of lips;
And scarlet, O scarlet
  The Wild Rose Hips!

Gay as a gipsy
  All Autumn long,
Here on the hedge-top
  This is my song.

The Rose Hip Fairy

The Ash Tree Fairy

◆ THE SONG OF ◆
THE ASH TREE FAIRY

Trunk and branches are smooth and grey;
  (Ash-grey, my honey!)
The buds of the Ash-tree, black are they;
    (And the days are long and sunny.)

The leaves make patterns against the sky,
  (Blue sky, my honey!)
And the keys in bunches hang on high;
    (To call them "keys" is funny!)

Each with its seed, the keys hang there,
  (Still there, my honey!)
When the leaves are gone
  and the woods are bare;
    (Short days may yet be sunny.)

◆ THE SONG OF ◆
THE PINE TREE FAIRY

A tall, tall tree is the Pine tree,
 With its trunk of bright red-brown—
The red of the merry squirrels
 Who go scampering up and down.

There are cones on the tall, tall Pine tree,
 With its needles sharp and green;
Small seeds in the cones are hidden,
 And they ripen there unseen.

The elves play games with the squirrels
 At the top of the tall, tall tree,
Throwing cones for the squirrels to nibble—
 I wish I were there to see!

The Pine Tree Fairy

The Privet Fairy

◆ THE SONG OF ◆
THE PRIVET FAIRY

Here in the wayside hedge I stand,
And look across the open land;
Rejoicing thus, unclipped and free,
I think how you must envy me,
O garden Privet, prim and neat,
With tidy gravel at your feet!

• THE SONG OF •
THE SYCAMORE FAIRY

Because my seeds have wings, you know,
   They fly away to earth;
And where they fall, why, there they grow—
   New Sycamores have birth!
Perhaps a score? Oh, hundreds more!
   Too many, people say!
And yet to me it's fun to see
   My winged seeds fly away.
(But first they must turn ripe and brown,
   And lose their flush of red;
And *then* they'll all go twirling down
   To earth, to find a bed.)

The Sycamore Fairy

The White Bryony Fairy

◆ THE SONG OF ◆
THE LIME TREE FAIRY

Bees! bees! come to the trees
Where the Lime has hung her treasures;
  Come, come, hover and hum;
  Come and enjoy your pleasures!
The feast is ready, the guests are bidden;
  Under the petals the honey is hidden;
Like pearls shine the drops of sweetness there,
And the scent of the Lime-flowers fills the air.
But soon these blossoms pretty and pale
Will all be gone; and the leaf-like sail
Will bear the little round fruits away;
  So bees! bees! come while you may!

◆ THE SONG OF ◆
THE WHITE BRYONY FAIRY

Have you seen at Autumn-time
Fairy-folk adorning
All the hedge with necklaces,
Early in the morning?
Green beads and red beads
Threaded on a vine:
Is there any handiwork
Prettier than mine?

The Lime Tree Fairy

The Alder Fairy

◆ THE SONG OF ◆
THE ALDER FAIRY

By the lake or river-side
   Where the Alders dwell,
In the Autumn may be spied
   Baby catkins; cones beside—
Old and new as well.
   Seasons come and seasons go;
That's the tale they tell!

After Autumn, Winter's cold
   Leads us to the Spring;
And, before the leaves unfold,
On the Alder you'll behold,
   Crimson catkins swing!
They are making ready now:
   That's the song I sing!

• THE SONG OF •
THE ELM TREE FAIRY

Soft and brown in Winter-time,
Dark and green in Summer's prime,
All their leaves a yellow haze
In the pleasant Autumn days—
See the lines of Elm trees stand
Keeping watch through all the land
Over lanes, and crops, and cows,
And the fields where Dobbin ploughs.
All day long, with listening ears,
Sits the Elm-tree Elf, and hears
Distant bell, and bleat, and bark,
Whistling boy, and singing lark.
Often on the topmost boughs
Many a rook has built a house;
Evening comes; and overhead,
Cawing, home they fly to bed.

The Elm Tree Fairy

The Sweet Chestnut Fairy

◆ THE SONG OF ◆
THE SWEET CHESTNUT FAIRY

Chestnuts, sweet Chestnuts,
　To pick up and eat,
Or keep until Winter,
　When, hot, they're a treat!

Like hedgehogs, their shells
　Are prickly outside;
But silky within,
　Where the little nuts hide,

Till the shell is split open,
　And, shiny and fat,
The Chestnut appears;
　Says the Fairy: "How's *that*?"

✦ THE SONG OF ✦
THE WILLOW FAIRY

By the peaceful stream or the shady pool
I dip my leaves in the water cool.

Over the water I lean all day,
Where the sticklebacks and the minnows play.

I dance, I dance, when the breezes blow,
And dip my toes in the stream below.

The Willow Fairy

The Cherry Tree Fairy

THE SONG OF
THE CHERRY TREE FAIRY

Cherries, a treat for the blackbirds;
 Cherries for girls and boys;
And there's never an elf in the treetops
 But cherries are what he enjoys!

Cherries in garden and orchard,
 Ripe and red in the sun;
And the merriest elf in the treetops
 Is the fortunate Cherry-tree one!

◆ THE SONG OF ◆
THE HAZEL-NUT FAIRY

Slowly, slowly, growing
　　While I watched them well,
See, my nuts have ripened;
　　Now I've news to tell.
I will tell the Squirrel,
　　"Here's a store for you;
But, kind Sir, remember
　　The Nuthatch likes them too."

I will tell the Nuthatch,
　　"Now, Sir, you may come;
Choose your nuts and crack them,
　　But leave the children some."
I will tell the children,
　　"You may take your share;
Come and fill your pockets,
　　But leave a few to spare."

The Hazel-Nut Fairy

The Holly Fairy

◆ THE SONG OF ◆
THE HOLLY FAIRY

O, I am green in Winter-time,
  When other trees are brown;
Of all the trees (So saith the rhyme)
  The holly bears the crown.
December days are drawing near
  When I shall come to town,
And carol-boys go singing clear
Of all the trees (O hush and hear!)
  The holly bears the crown!

For who so well-beloved and merry
As the scarlet Holly Berry?

◆ THE SONG OF ◆
THE SILVER BIRCH FAIRY

There's a gentle tree with a satiny bark,
All silver-white, and upon it, dark,
Is many a crosswise line and mark—
    She's a tree there's no mistaking!
The Birch is this light and lovely tree,
And as light and lovely still is she
When the Summer's time has come to flee,
    As she was at Spring's awaking.

She has new Birch-catkins, small and tight,
Though the old ones scatter
    and take their flight,
And the little leaves, all yellow and bright,
    In the autumn winds are shaking.
And with fluttering wings
    and hands that cling,
The fairies play and the fairies swing
On the fine thin twigs,
    that will toss and spring
      With never a fear of breaking.

The Silver Birch Fairy

The Box Tree Fairy

◆ THE SONG OF ◆
THE BOX TREE FAIRY

Have you seen the Box unclipped,
Never shaped and never snipped?
Often it's a garden hedge,
Just a narrow little edge;
Or in funny shapes it's cut,
And it's very pretty; *but*—

But, unclipped, it is a tree,
Growing as it likes to be;
And it has its blossoms too;
Tiny buds, the Winter through,
Wait to open in the Spring
In a scented yellow ring.

And among its leaves there play
Little blue-tits, brisk and gay.

✦ THE SONG OF ✦
THE RIBWORT PLANTAIN FAIRY

Hullo, Snailey-O!
How's the world with *you*?
Put your little horns out;
Tell me how you do?
There's rain, and dust, and sunshine,
Where carts go creaking by;
You like it wet, Snailey;
I like it dry!

Hey ho, Snailey-O,
I'll whistle you a tune!
I'm merry in September
As e'er I am in June.
By any stony roadside
Wherever you may roam,
All the summer through, Snailey,
Plantain's at home!

The Ribwort Plantain Fairy

The Horse Chestnut Fairy

• THE SONG OF •
THE HORSE CHESTNUT FAIRY

My conkers, they are shiny things,
 And things of mighty joy,
And they are like the wealth of kings
 To every little boy;
I see the upturned face of each
 Who stands around the tree:
He sees his treasure out of reach,
 But does not notice *me*.

For love of conkers bright and brown,
 He pelts the tree all day;
With stones and sticks he knocks them down,
 And thinks it jolly play.
But sometimes I, the elf, am hit
 Until I'm black and blue;
O laddies, only wait a bit,
 I'll shake them down to you!

◆ THE SONG OF ◆
THE NIGHTSHADE BERRY FAIRY

"You see my berries, how they gleam and
glow,
Clear ruby-red, and green, and orange-
yellow;
Do they not tempt you, fairies, dangling so?"
The fairies shake their heads and answer "No!
You are a crafty fellow!"

"What, won't you try them? There is
naught to pay!
Why should you think my berries poisoned
things?
You fairies may look scared and fly away—
The children will believe me when I say
My fruit is fruit for kings!"
But all good fairies cry in anxious haste,
"O children, do not taste!"

The Nightshade Berry Fairy

The Plane Tree Fairy

◆ THE SONG OF ◆
THE PLANE TREE FAIRY

You will not find him in the wood,
    Nor in the country lane;
But in the city's parks and streets
    You'll see the Plane.

O turn your eyes from pavements grey,
    And look you up instead,
To where the Plane tree's pretty balls
    Hang overhead!

When he has shed his golden leaves,
    His balls will yet remain,
To deck the tree until the Spring
    Comes back again!

✦ THE SONG OF ✦
THE MULBERRY FAIRY

"Here we go round the Mulberry bush!"
You remember the rhyme—oh yes!
But which of you know
How Mulberries grow
On the slender branches, drooping low?
Not many of you, I guess.

Someone goes round the Mulberry bush
When nobody's there to see;
He takes the best
And he leaves the rest,
From top to toe like a Mulberry drest:
This fat little fairy's he!

The Mulberry Fairy

The Burdock Fairy

◆ THE SONG OF ◆
THE BURDOCK FAIRY

Wee little hooks on each brown little bur,
(Mind where you're going, O Madam and Sir!)
How they will cling to your skirt-hem and stocking!
Hear how the Burdock is laughing and mocking:
Try to get rid of me, try as you will,
Shake me and scold me, I'll stick to you still,
    I'll stick to you still!

◆ THE SONG OF ◆
THE YEW FAIRY

Here, on the dark and solemn Yew,
   A marvel may be seen,
Where waxen berries, pink and new,
   Appear amid the green.

I sit a-dreaming in the tree,
   So old and yet so new;
One hundred years, or two, or three
   Are little to the Yew.

I think of bygone centuries,
   And seem to see anew
The archers face their enemies
   With bended bows of Yew.

The Yew Fairy

Other Titles in **th**is series: